Bubblelina

IN: A FROZEN DISCOVERY
BY: CHRISTINA LEE JOHNSON
AKA "QUEEN TINA"

NOBODY MOVE
THIS IS A STICK UP!

HAND OVER THE MONEY!

WHAT!?!

YOUR WITHDRAWAL
IS CANCELLED!

BUBBLELINA STOPS
BANK ROBBERY

BUBBLELINA SAVES SIX YEAR
OLD BOY FROM DROWNING.

BUBBLELINA SAVES A
BABY FROM A HOUSE FIRE

Wow, Bubblelina really gets around! She's like a real life version of Deep Sea Girl...
THE PASADENA TIMES
WHO IS BUBBLELINA?
Witnesses say Bubblelina is the protector of the land and sea. For several weeks since Bubblelina arrived, she saved people from monsterous sharks, and managed to save the students from Carver Middle School from an octopus at the Long Beach Aquarium. Two
Bubblelina rescued Jarvis Miller His family was grat
Before rescusing little Jarvis, Bubblelina managed to stop a robbery at the First Bank of Pasadena.
Then Bubblelina managed to save Chen Yang from drowning at the Santa Monica Pier where she made her first appearance.
Many
very
want
as wo

... but younger and more adorable. I wouldn't mind having Bubblelina as my girlfriend!

Gosh, William you're something else. I'm starting to get tired of hearing the news about Bubblelina. My main focus is how well I did on the math test and waiting for the entire day to be over.

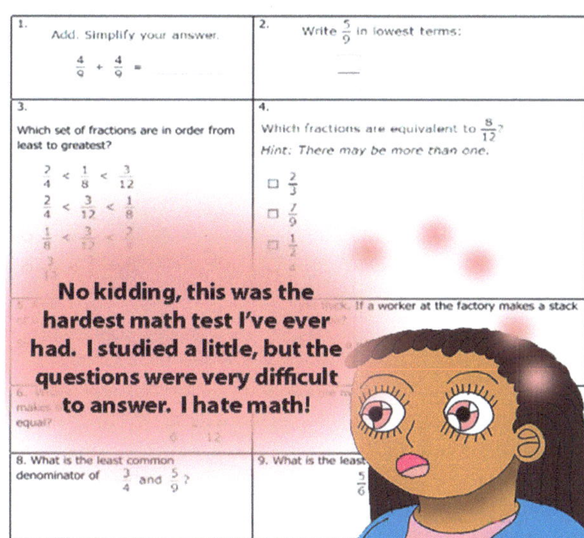

No kidding, this was the hardest math test I've ever had. I studied a little, but the questions were very difficult to answer. I hate math!

I believe I did good on my test!
William, you have always been good at math. They should call you, "The Math Genius."
And science too!

WELL THAT MAKES ME, "THE MATH AND SCIENCE GENIUS!"

I wonder who that girl is sitting all alone?
I really don't know, but I overheard people in the hallway say that she is the smartest girl in school.

We're both in the science club, but I never got a chance to talk to her because I've been so busy with all of my class assignments. I rarely see her eat in the cafeteria. She's always by herself whenever I do see her.

Well, I'm going to sit with her, so I can get to know her better.

HELLO THERE!

Um, hello?

Allow me to introduce myself. My name is Melissa Doris Robinson and I'm in the sixth grade.

My name is Vanessa, Vanessa Anna Summerfield, and I'm also in the sixth grade.

You look like you could use a friend. Why are you always alone at school?

I used to be home schooled when I was in elementary school until my parents decided to send me to a public school so that I could work on my social skills and get to know new people.

Well, I haven't made any friends at all because I am more focused on my studies.
Math

Being alone is good sometimes, but it doesn't hurt to have friends. Having friends is the beauty of making your life fun and exciting! Do you have any sisters or brothers?

I am adopted. My dad's a doctor and my mom's a nurse. I have an older brother named Michael who is in college majoring in the medical field. I want to be a doctor as well when I grow up and follow in my parents' footsteps.

You're in a family of doctors. That's wonderful! Guess what?! I'm adopted too! My dad owns a restaurant called Robinson's Grill. My mom works from home by doing DIY videos on the Internet. My mom is the one who makes most of my clothes. She made the outfit I'm wearing now.

It looks beautiful and pretty on you. I've never became much of a fashion type. Most of the clothes in my closet lacks color, so I mostly wear black and white. I wish I had your taste in style.
If you are interested, I could let you wear some of my clothes.

Well, about your clothes, I um… don't think I'll be able to wear them.

Well, well, well if it isn't little Melissa and some random bookworm.
What do you want Elisha? We're not in the mood for your insults! Why don't you go to the library and read a fashion magazine or something!

Let me guess, you dissed chubby Nicole and William the King of Dorks…

… for this loner with a puffy afro. Judging by the look of you, you seem too short to be in middle school. What's your name little girl?

Vanessa Summerfield, and I am not a little girl! I'M IN THE SIXTH GRADE YOU BULLY!

Oh I'm so sorry. I didn't mean to be a bully to you. I should be nicer. Your clothes are very nice, but…

… they make you look like my grandmother, and afros are out. You need to hang around people with style, instead of a mop-head like Melissa, unless you prefer looking like a Mini-Granny.

QUIT INSULTING US! I AM NOT A MOP HEAD! DON'T YOU HAVE SOMETHING BETTER TO DO THAN MAKE JUST FUN OF US, MISS PRISSY PANTS! THERE ARE TIMES THAT I WANT TO PULL YOUR HAIR REALLY HARD AND TIE YOU ONTO A CEILING FAN SO THAT YOU CAN SPIN ALL AROUND THE CAFETERIA!

LOOKS LIKE YOU WANT TO PICK A FIGHT WITH ME! I HATE TO BREAK IT TO YOU HONEY, BUT I'M GOING TO WIN ANYWAY SINCE I AM STRONGER AND BETTER THAN YOU!

I'VE HAD ENOUGH OF YOU!
BRING IT ON!

GGGGGGGRRRRRRRR!!!!!!!!!!!!!!!!!

STOP IT, BOTH OF YOU!

I think we should go, before we make a scene and get in trouble.

What a bunch of losers!

MEANWHILE AT SERENA'S LAIR

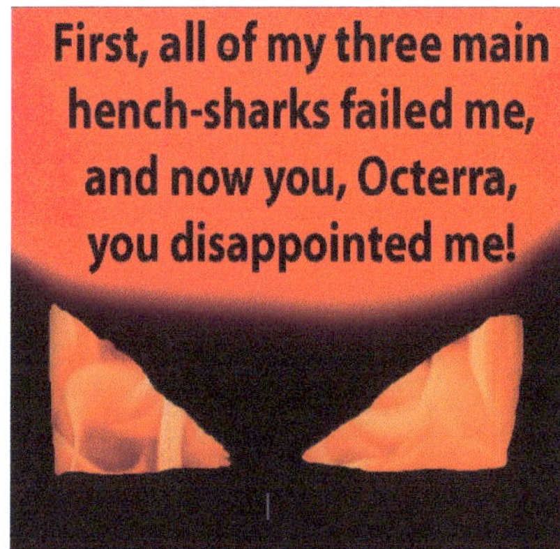

First, all of my three main hench-sharks failed me, and now you, Octerra, you disappointed me!

With all do respect my lady, I was so close to getting that Bubblelina brat until she erased the spell of my octopus. One of these days she will pay and I will get my revenge.

You look more eager to get Bubblelina, so I'm still letting you stay. Now who wants to stop Bubblelina next?

I WILL!

Well, Orca you know what to do! Stop Bubblelina no matter what it takes!

It will be my ultimate pleasure!

Back at school

I can't believe you have to put up with this girl. What was her name again?
Elisha. I try my best to avoid her but she keeps on finding me, especially when I'm hanging out with Chris.
Who is Chris?

Chris is the most cutest and popular boy in the seventh grade, and I really have a crush on him. Almost every night, I have dreams about him.
LIONS
14

There is one dream that I was a mermaid. I saw Chris underwater unconscious and saved him.

We'd almost kissed, until my alarm clock woke up.

If I get a chance to know him better, maybe we could be more than just friends.

Chris sounds like a sweet guy. He has the cutest hair and eyes I've ever seen.
That's the two best things that I like about Chris, his curly black hair and his sparkling blue eyes.

Since we both just met today, do you want to hang out after school?
I would, but I have to go to the beach with a student that I'm helping out with her science report about whales.
Okay, maybe some other time, nice meeting you.

Nice meeting you too!

Later that day at the beach.

Look Vaneesa! There's a killer whale doing a high jump!
That is one interesting killer whale.

While you continue observing and taking notes for your science report, do you want something to drink Sarah?
Sure, I'll take a nice cold pink lemonade.
Alright, I'll be right back.
Okay.

They're so cool!

MWAHAHAHAHAHAHA!!!!!!!!!!!

VANEESA, HELP!!!

IT'S A MONSTER!!!
AND IT'S GOT THAT LITTLE GIRL!!!
SARAH!!!

MWHAHAHAHAHAHA!!!!!!

I DON'T KNOW WHO OR WHAT YOU ARE, BUT YOU BETTER LET SARAH GO NOW!!!

I DON'T THINK SO LITTLE GIRL!!!

OH NO!!!

SOMEBODY PLEASE HELP!!! HELP!!!
THAT VOICE SOUNDS LIKE VANESSA AND SHE'S IN TROUBLE!

ZIP!!!

MAGICAL BUBBLE POWER!!!

What is it, young lady?!

A half-woman, half-whale captured Sarah!

Don't worry, I'll save her!

Now that I trapped you, maybe Bubblelina would come to rescue you and once she comes, she will be mine to bring to Serena!

How dare you trap an innocent little girl. She and the children all around the world represent our future. I am Bubblelina, protector of the sea and land and you will be stopped!

So you are Bubblelina! Well, you are going to be tied up with this little guppy.

SUPER BUBBLE BARRAGE!

I DON'T THINK SO!!!

I wish that I had the courage and strength like Bubblelina in order to save Sarah, but I can't swim.

Sarah's life is in danger and there are times that you have to conquer your fears in order to save someone in need.

WHAT IN THE WORLD?!

ZIP!!!!

Did I just turn into a mermaid or is it just my imagination?

Yes, and I am the queen of Coralona. Also, you were born a mermaid by the name Odetta and your real parents died at birth from the destruction of Coralona by the evil sea witch, Serena and I transferred all of the born and unborn babies to different parts of the world to loving human families who would care for them. I would explain the rest later, but I want you to have this.

Yes, and I am the queen of Coralona. Also, you were born a mermaid by the name Odetta and your real parents died at birth from the destruction of Coralona by the evil sea witch, Serena and I transferred all of the born and unborn babies to different parts of the world to loving human families who would care for them. I would explain the rest later, but I want you to have this.

Here is your transformation shell, which will transform you into your true form as Odetta with magical ice powers. All you have to do is hold it up to the sky and say MAGICAL ICE POWER.

Okay I hope this helps.
MAGICAL ICE POWER!

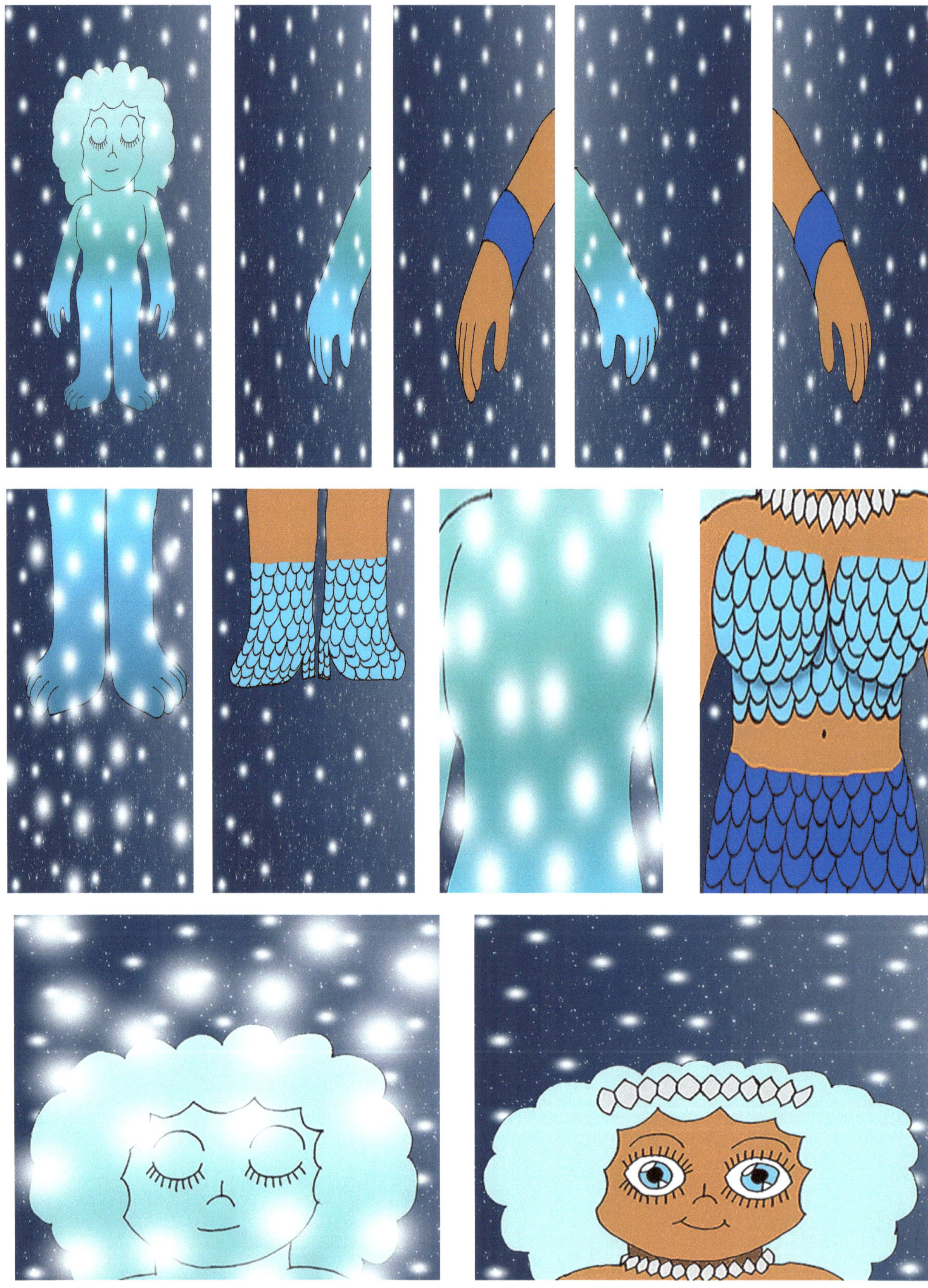

Wow! This is unbelievable! I transformed into a superhero with fish scales! Now, if you excuse me I have some important business I need to take care of!
Looks like capturing you, Bubblelina was easier for me, along with Miss Ponytail as a bonus. Too bad that octopus and those shark stooges couldn't pull this off!

Excuse me ugly whale creature! This little girl doesn't belong to you, and how dare you capture Bubblelina! I order you to let both of them go!
Who said that?

My name is Odetta, and I order you to let Bubblelina and this girl go, or you will have to deal with me!

Quick, Bubblelina as soon as I free you, tell Odetta to say, "FREEZING ICE BLIZZARD" in order to freze Orca. Then you can trap her with your BUBBLE SPHERE. I'll get Sarah to the surface.
Okay.

Odetta you got to say FREEZING ICE BLIZZARD, now!!

Okay, FREEZING ICE BLIZZARD!

SNATCH!!!

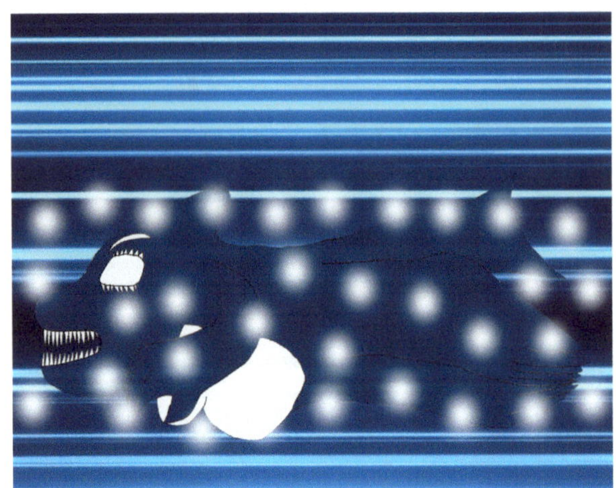
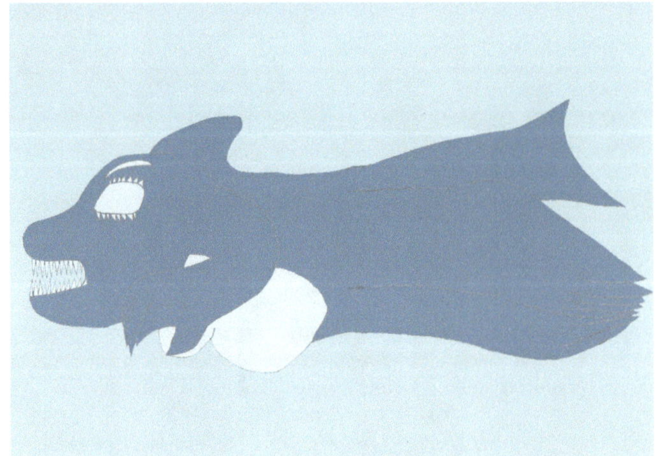

PUNCH!

WE DID IT! WE DID IT!
INDEED. NOW LET'S GO BACK TO SHORE.

BACK AT SERENA'S LAIR

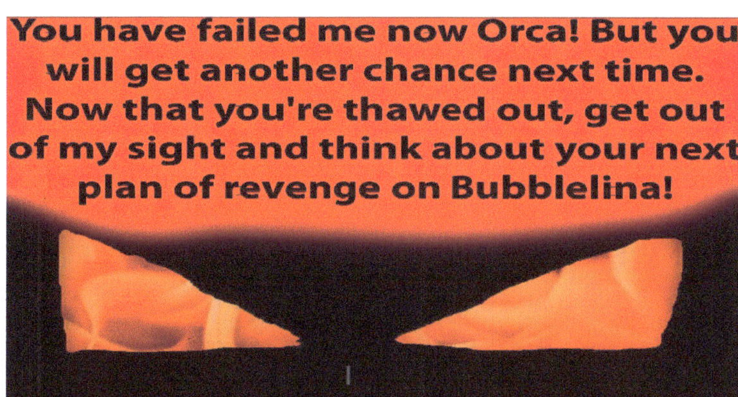

You have failed me now Orca! But you will get another chance next time. Now that you're thawed out, get out of my sight and think about your next plan of revenge on Bubblelina!

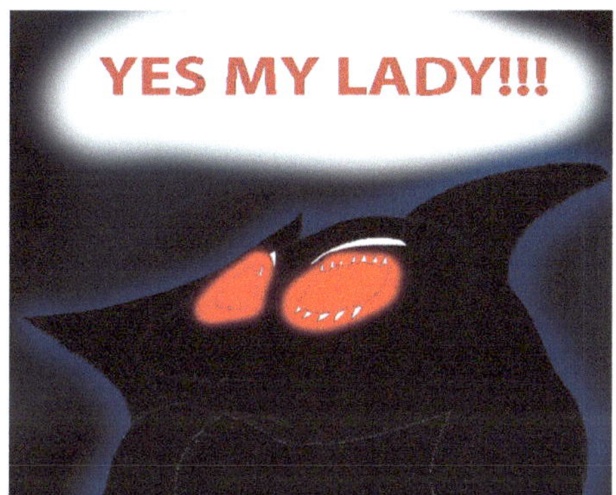

YES MY LADY!!!

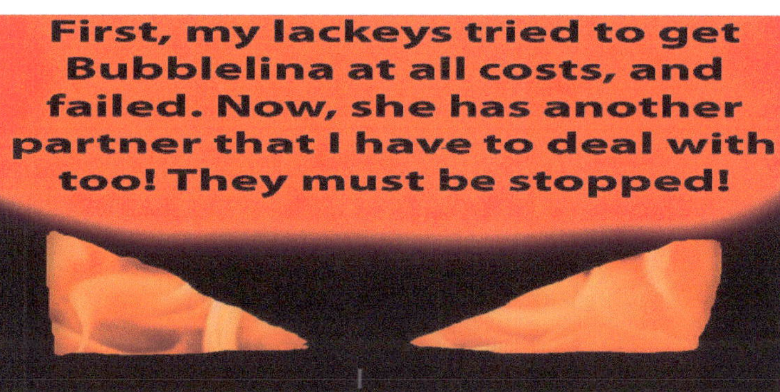

First, my lackeys tried to get Bubblelina at all costs, and failed. Now, she has another partner that I have to deal with too! They must be stopped!

Melissa?!
You are Bubblelina
this whole time!

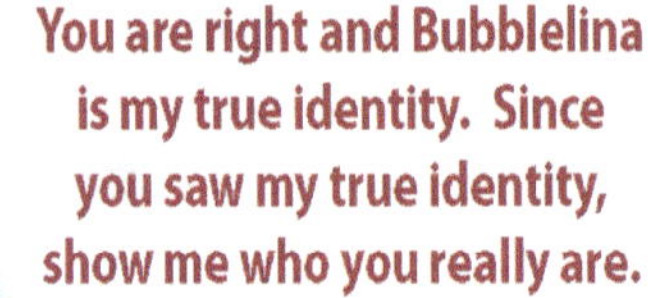

You are right and Bubblelina
is my true identity. Since
you saw my true identity,
show me who you really are.

VANESSA! I can't
believe that you
are a mermaid
superhero too! I
just find this hard
to believe.

I had a hard time
believing until Queen
Nerissa told me. I'm
guessing that Nerissa
is your birth mother
since the both of you
look so much alike.

You got that right! Since we are both
partners fighting for what's right in order to
restore Coralona, there is one rule you must
follow and obey, never tell and reveal your
secret identity to anyone. That includes your
close friends and family members.

YIPPEE! Looks like this is going to be the beginning of a beautiful heroic friendship.

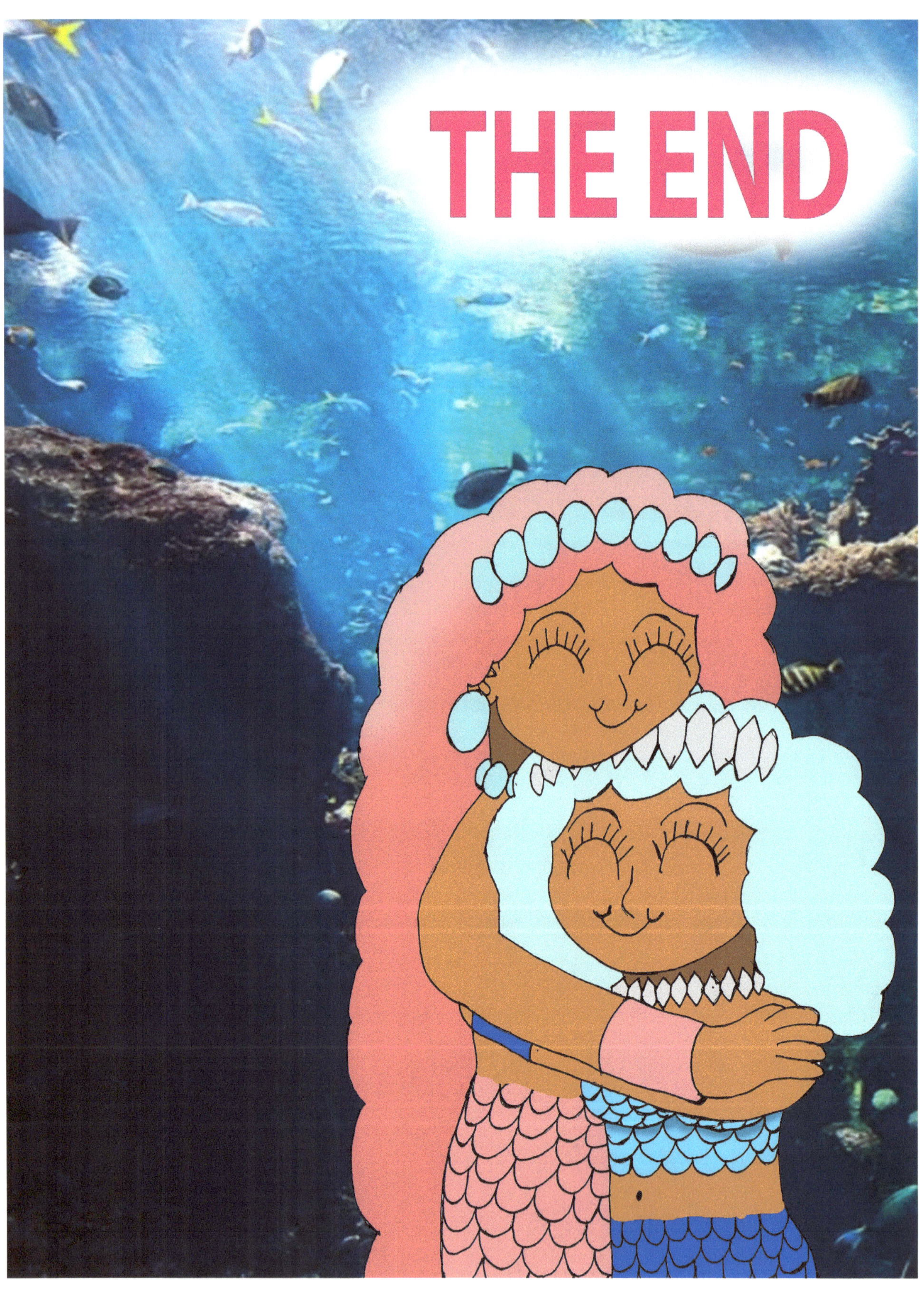
THE END

SPECIAL THANKS TO JESUS CHRIST,
HIS FATHER JEHOVAH GOD, AND
ALL MY SUPPORTING FAMILY AND
FRIENDS FOR EVERYTHING THAT
HELP ME MAKE THIS COMIC AND
MANY MORE TO COME!

Enter multiple universes with magical plush toys, magicians, mystical warriors, superheroes, mermaids, fairies, and so much more!

Email us at miraclecomics6776@gmail.com or call or text (318)422-6203 to order the comic books.

Watch videos on our Youtube channel and subscribe!
https://youtube.com/channel/UC1qBO6WpDdhJAOEyZONsA

And support us on Patreon at
https://www.patreon.com/user?u=61396551

www.ingramcontent.com/pod-product-compliance
Lightning Source LLC
Chambersburg PA
CBHW042123110726
48006CB00003B/746